Baby Cat

By Dawn McMillan
Illustrated by Rae Dale

"Here, Kitty!" said Annie.

"I'm going to play with you today.

You are going to be my baby.

"Here is your baby hat.

Here is your bed.

It is time to go to sleep."

"You are a good baby.
Stay in your bed!" said Annie.

"Look, Mum!
Come and see my baby.
He is asleep.
Look at his little head,
and his little nose,
and his big feet."

Mum looked at Kitty.
His tail went up and down.

"Kitty is not happy," said Mum.
"He is going to wake up."

Kitty jumped up!

He jumped up and over the table,
up and over the chair,
and went down under the bed.

Annie looked under the bed.

"Come here, Kitty!" she said.

"It is time for dinner.

You will be hungry.

Come on, Kitty! Come on!"

Kitty did not come.

Annie got Kitty's dinner.

"Come here, Kitty!" she said.

"Fish! Fish!"

Kitty came for his fish.

"You **are** hungry,"
said Annie.

"You are a good cat," said Annie.
"Stay here with me.
I'm going to take off
your hat."

Kitty went back to eating his fish.

"My baby is a cat again,"
said Annie.